O2

KELLYN SOLVERA

Copyright © 2024 by Kellyn Solvera

All rights reserved.

No part of this book may be reproduced or transmitted in any form or by any means, electronic or mechanical, except for the purpose of review and/or reference, without explicit permission in writing from the publisher.

Cover design copyright © 2024 by Niki Lenhart
nikilen-designs.com

Published by Water Dragon Publishing
waterdragonpublishing.com

ISBN 978-1-962538-39-8 (Trade Paperback)

FIRST EDITION

10 9 8 7 6 5 4 3 2 1

AUTHOR'S NOTE

Sometimes we ask ourselves whether we take things like the air we breathe for granted. On a chilly, gray Christmas Day not long ago, this question came to me on a tram crossing the Danube River, and I tried to imagine a scenario where the air we breathe has become rare and precious. Kōbō Abe's novel, *Woman in the Dunes*, also came to mind. But rather than scheming villagers who lure victims into a life of extreme constraint where they must toil for survival, humanity creates this situation.

02

"EVERY DAY HE'LL CONSUME 550 liters of oxygen, four liters of water, 40 grams of protein, 1800 calories — no, he's big. 2000. Can we get the allocations?"

"He's waking up," said a second female voice. "Mr. Morton, can you hear me? Squeeze my hand if you can."

"Where's Lydia?" I mumbled.

"Who's Lydia?" asked the first female voice.

"My wife."

"John, you were in suspended animation," the second voice said. "The year is 2247."

"Yes," I replied, groping to comprehend these first sounds, first voices, I had heard in more than two centuries.

"But your wife and everyone else from that time is gone."

Minutes later, I opened my eyes to bright operating room lights. Tubes were connected to my veins. I was shivering cold. Two women in surgical gowns and masks were standing over me.

"Complete the warming process," said the one with straight dark hair who told me the year. The other woman turned a valve on one of the fluid bags, and I felt warmth coursing up one of my arms.

"Wha... wha... what about my ... my ... lymphoma?" I stammered.

"It's cured," the dark-haired woman replied. "We kept you asleep until we did."

Other memories returned along with rudimentary cogitation. "How ... how ... many other frozen ... frozen cancer persons have ... have you ... you cured?"

The women exchanged glances.

"You're the first," the dark haired one replied,

"How ... how many ... many you try ... before ... before me?"

Again they paused and exchanged glances. "... Three."

"They all ...?"

"Yes. Thawing has been the big challenge. Most of the cryopreservation fluids just didn't work. Fortunately, in your case, they used an unusual type that protected your cells well enough, but whose toxic effects we could counteract ... That's a lot to take in ... Did you understand?"

"Understand," I murmured.

"Actually, Dr. Kovacs here not only figured out a cure for your disease," said the other woman, "she also found a way to overcome the side effects of that unusual preservation fluid."

My mind began to clear. "My wife ... she was also sick. ... She ... she probably was frozen, too ... just after me. ... What happened to her."

"I'll have to see if I can find anything out," Dr. Kovacs replied brusquely, with an expression indicating I was imposing on her time. I figured an answer would take days.

My robotically controlled gurney moved silently out of the operating room down a corridor and into an ICU. Later that day, Dr. Kovacs came to check on my condition. Expressing satisfaction with my progress, I was surprised when she added, "Mr. Morton, I've examined logs of all the cryopreservation laboratories over the past two hundred twenty-two years. There is no one that fits your wife's name or birthday. However," she continued with a touch of sympathy softening her stern demeanor, "a woman who fits all these died in a nursing home in Connecticut at age 92. Here are copies of her death and cremation certificates." Her name at death was Lydia Morton.

Groggy as I was, I remember my hope vanishing and my energy draining away. I managed to murmur, "I'm happy she lived a long life,. But my incoherent feelings, that I only later put into words, were, *What is there to live for now? It would have been better if I had remained frozen — my last memories having been of being surrounded by my family as I was put peacefully to sleep.*

"Mr. Morton, a lot has changed over the past two hundred twenty years," Dr. Kovacs said. "We can talk about this later. But tomorrow, we need to put you to sleep one more time to clear the remaining preservation fluid and help your cells adjust to a normal environment. Then we will keep you sedated a couple more days as all the synapses between your brain cells gradually reactivate."

They must not have used enough anesthetic during that procedure the next day. Although groggy, I could hear the same two women talking. From this conversation, It seemed Dr. Kovacs was the team leader, and her colleague was Dr. Williams.

"What are we going to do with him?" Dr. Williams asked.

"I managed to get him allocations of oxygen, water, calories, protein," replied Dr. Kovacs.

"Where will he stay? What will he do? He was a physical therapist, but we have no energy to waste on exercise." After some moments of silence, Dr. Williams continued. "Hanna, you're one of my best friends, I hope you consider me the same. But was it scientific curiosity … or desire for achievement — curing a rare disease and bringing someone back from the dead?"

"Maybe he could help our patients deal with things like bone loss, muscle atrophy. Especially men, who suffer more from nutritional deprivation."

"You still thinking of Sebastian? … Sorry, didn't mean to go there."

Again, silence. Dr. Kovacs cleared her throat, "It was a different world back then. So wasteful … so fun."

"You want to bring a bit of that world to ours?"

The anesthetic finally took full effect and I lost consciousness. After the procedure ended and the anesthetic wore off, there followed a day of vivid, bizarre, terrifying dreams, then a day of peaceful sleep. The next day, I must have still been sedated, for my head felt airy and I was not motivated to do anything. I was visited by psychologists who asked questions to test my memory and reasoning. Then came physical therapists who had me move different parts of my body, then stand, then shuffle, and finally walk around the room.

The next day, Dr. Kovacs and Dr. Williams, along with nurses, department chiefs, and the hospital Director gathered around my bed. The Director ordered me to get out of bed, move various muscles, describe recent events and also events from my time. Then they congratulated Dr. Kovacs. Everyone was beaming except Dr. Kovacs, who regarded me pensively.

As people dispersed, the Director came up to me and, in a low voice, said that space was needed in the hospital for other patients, and I was to be discharged the next day to the care of Dr. Kovacs in her apartment. I looked at him in surprise, and then glanced at Dr. Kovacs, who remained expressionless.

"Don't worry," the Director said. "In our era, housing is so short many people must accept living arrangements that might have been considered, well, unorthodox in your day. Dr. Kovacs is one of our most capable physicians. She will treat you professionally." Saying this, he glanced at Dr. Kovacs, who met his glance impassively. "And of course, you'll come back here frequently for checkups. It's not as if the hospital is saying good-bye and shutting its doors to you." He shook my hand and stepped away to speak with Dr. Kovacs.

Dr Williams approached. "The Director's right. Also, Dr. Kovacs's apartment is large. One of the best places you could stay, and you're being there will help her keep it."

That afternoon, I explored the hospital for the first time. From the windows I saw just ocean, except for a few other islands with tall buildings covering each one. *I am alone in a strange world. They say it's changed a lot, but how? Everyone I knew is gone. Now I will have to live with a reticent stranger who holds power of life or death over me.*

These concerns were not eased when Dr. Kovacs hurried into my room the next day, two hours late for my scheduled discharge. She seemed preoccupied, and when I asked about what I has seen from the windows, she simply said, "You'll soon see."

•   •   •

The elevator in the middle of the hospital complex descended, stopped, underwent muffled shakes as latches above and below disengaged and reengaged, then moved horizontally underground. We exited onto a platform with plain, white-tiled walls. From our left a shining, white train with no traces of graffiti appeared. Dr. Kovacs motioned me to sit next to her. Like her, the other passengers appeared underweight and fatigued. I must have stood out as one of the most robust.

The train accelerated smoothly, traveling through an underwater tunnel whose walls were of glass or clear plastic. The water was murky, but the tunnel seemed to be resting on a roadway. Signs flashed by: *Exit 61 Patchoque, Exit 60 Sayville.*

"Hey, this is the Long Island Expressway!" I blurted out.

Passengers stared. Dr. Kovacs waved them off. "He's not from around here." Then in a low voice she asked, "You know this area?"

"My parents live, I mean lived, near here."

"Then you knew about Suffolk County Community College?" I nodded. "The hospital is on the hill where it stood."

The tracks suddenly rose above the water, and the train stopped on a platform atop a low isthmus barely above sea level. A platform sign read, *Station closed frequently due to storm surges and high winds.*

"We transfer here," Dr Kovacs said.

The sign above the exit door read, West Hills Station. *My God!* I thought, *the house where I grew up is near here.*

We rode a monorail which climbed up what was a nature preserve in my day, but now the cars wound their way through canyons between soaring apartment blocks.

The monorail made a sharp turn and we exited at Jayne's Hill Station into a covered indoor arcade with low ceilings and shops with subdued lighting. On one side of our corridor at the bottom of an airspace between two apartment blocks was a small Japanese rock garden. A lone couple sat in the garden wearing masks connected to small oxygen cylinders they wore as backpacks. Dr Kovacs noticed them, too.

"The amount of oxygen outside is only a third of what it was in your day, like it was on top of Mount Everest back then. Before people go out, they must put on oxygen tanks and masks."

"What happened to the oxygen?"

"Acid rain and heat killed land plants. Then most ocean organisms died from sea warming and acidification. All the dead organisms caused ocean oxygen levels to fall further in a vicious cycle. But land vegetation is slowly recovering – actually doing pretty well in Antarctica. We think ocean levels of phytoplankton are stabilizing."

"So things are getting better."

"Gradually ... won't notice a difference in my lifetime, nor in yours ... unless you get cryopreserved again. ... And for millennia, ocean levels will remain almost seventy meters higher than in your day."

We rode an elevator to the 43rd floor. She peered into an iris-scanning sensor to unlock her door. As she opened it, she paused, saying, "Welcome, please call me Hanna."

Her apartment was long and narrow, no more than two meters wide and fifteen meters deep. I was immediately drawn to the north-facing window at the end of the apartment. In the far distance I could make out the Connecticut coastline. Hanna handed me a pair of binoculars from the window ledge. There was no sign of Stamford, Norwalk Bridgeport and New Haven. All were submerged.

"What happened to all the people who used to live along the Connecticut coast?" I asked.

"Some were able to move inland. But it was chaotic. Many didn't make it. ... But that was generations ago."

Then straight in front, just above the shoreline, I recognized the Town Hall of my hometown, Wilton, surrounded by buildings I did not recognize. I pointed this out to Hanna. "It was a beautiful town, nestled among tree-covered hills. Every house had a nearby pond where couples could stroll, and children play ... I wonder what it's like now."

At Hanna's invitation, we sat down at a small table for tea and some hard biscuits. At first we avoided each other's glances.

"So, I'm here as an experiment?"

"No. ... I mean, well, ... yes. We wanted to know if we could revive someone who had been frozen. I knew a way it might be done. But there'd be just one chance.

All over the world, the capsules are being deactivated. I thought, *Can't we try to save just one? If we succeed, we will know how to help future patients.*"

"What do you mean?"

"Power is being cut off to the cryopreservation capsules."

"But that's hundreds of people."

"It has to be done to save energy."

"Why did you pick me?"

There was a long pause. "Well ... I was pretty sure I could cure your lymphoma and reverse the effects of the preservation solution. Otherwise, you were fit, more likely to survive ... and ..."

"And what?"

"You had refused the procedure vehemently, despite your parents' begging you to have it and offering to pay the costs. Then, with only a few weeks to live, you changed your mind. Your last recorded message to your kids was, 'I am doing this so mama can live.' I was intrigued by what that meant."

I had to pause before answering: "Lydia, my wife, also became gravely ill soon after my lymphoma entered its terminal stage. The only therapy for her was very risky, experimental. Our insurance wouldn't cover it. One of the specialists we consulted said that cryopreservation with me would be a better option. Then my parents stepped in.

"They had not spoken to Lydia since we were married, never seen our kids. They were proud, considered her beneath my family. They disowned me when we got married. But Lydia and I made our marriage work. I put her through school. She started to earn good money. Then she didn't want to have anything to do with my folks.

"Now they were suddenly promising to pay either the cost of her therapy or cryopreservation, whichever she chose; and they promised to take care of our children if anything should happen to her. But they begged me to have the procedure, and Lydia said she wouldn't accept any treatment unless I underwent cryopreservation. So I agreed. The last thing I remember was her holding my hand and saying, 'We will be together again.' …

"You told me back in the hospital that she passed away in a nursing home in Wilton when she was 92."

"Yes, 168 years ago."

Embarrassed by the silence and the tears coming to my eyes, I said, "Too bad I can't show you photos. I had them on my phone which was in a pouch secured to the cryopreservation capsule." Hanna reached into her hospital bag which she had placed on the table and removed what seemed like a small tablet computer.

"We managed to back up the contents of your phone onto this. … Touch the screen. It should work like your phone." I did. A colorful display announced it was 6:10 pm, Friday, June 4th, 2247. I shifted my eyes and the screen changed to show my oxygen, water, protein and calorie allocations for the day and which production plants or warehouses supplied each. "Don't worry about those," Hanna said. "They appear automatically on every person's device." I again glanced at the margin and the sign-in screen on my old phone appeared. I entered my 222-year-old password and familiar screens appeared. My heart raced as I touched the photo icon and scrolled through the photos.

"Here, this was the last Holiday season we had together," I exclaimed unable to suppress the excitement and anxiety in my voice. "We were still in good health. They're at our kitchen table in Wilton making Christmas cookies and cakes. This is Lydia. She's laughing so hard about some joke Jeremy and Heather just made. Jeremy's 13, Heather 8. Little Yvonne here is two, leaning over her highchair trying to spread icing on her own."

"What a nice family. Lydia and your kids seem so happy." Then I saw water filling Hanna's eyes.

"What's up?"

"Would you like to know what happened to your children?"

"Of course," I replied hesitantly.

"Yesterday I found these records," Hanna said passing them to me. I read the first sentence of a report compiled by the town government: 'Jeremy Morton (68), Heather Greenberg (63, né Morton), Yvonne Cranston (57, né Morton) died yesterday in their childhood home in Wilton during the rioting and ensuing fires.'

"It names many other persons who perished that day," Hanna continued, "about a year after your wife died."

The grief of parents who outlive their children swept over me. But inexplicably, I felt a twinge of morbid satisfaction in having foreseen this. Lydia and I often said to one another, "We may not be around to experience the effects of what we're doing to our planet, but our children will."

Now I am here in the future, I thought, *and the horrors we matter-of-factly contemplated for our children came to pass. But somehow, I survived to comprehend their fates.*

Hanna was also staring at the photo, and I wondered if she had any idea of the thoughts passing through my mind.

"You must miss them terribly," she said; then after a pause, "What a big, bright kitchen you had ... That brightly lit star taking up an entire window, the jars filled with flour, sugar, milk ... such things don't exist anymore ... This is my kitchen," she said gesturing to a bare metal countertop with two burners along the wall just two steps away from our little table. "Come, it's time to fix dinner."

From a small metal cupboard, Hanna took plastic containers of buckwheat and couscous. She browned the grains, added some water, and let them simmer as she stir-fried a small onion with a half-slice of pimento on the other burner. "For special occasions," she said, gesturing to the pimento. She mixed all the ingredients and divided the mixture into two plates. From a jar in her small refrigerator, she scooped two tablespoons of a dark brown paste atop the stir-fried mixture. I could identify sliced mushrooms inside.

"What's this," I asked, pointing to the topping.

"Try it first."

The overall texture was like the couscous, a bit saltier, with umami flavor and fine crunchiness. Whatever it was, the mushrooms complemented it well.

"This is one of the largest apartments," Hanna said diverting attention from the meal. "But everyone has the basics, including clean water and a place to stand and shower. Though, if you want more than one hot shower a week, you have to pay a lot."

"The topping was good," I said.

"Really? Well, you recognized the mushrooms. The rest ... insects." I didn't flinch. I had guessed as much. "It is all I have. It is the only animal protein any of us has ever known."

"It's good, really. Thank you … for saving my life and giving me a place to stay."

I felt tired. "You need rest," Hanna said as prepared her couch as a bed for me. "Your body is still adjusting to all the changes it's been through … Would you like some music before you sleep?"

"Sure, what do you like?"

"I like the hits from your era." From a sound system embedded in the walls, songs emerged that made it seem I was back in my own time. First there was *Lucky* by Mraz and Caillat, then *Count on Me* by Bruno Mars. So familiar and clear was the music that I felt I had only to walk out of this dark, narrow room and back into my den in Wilton, and everything would be the same.

"Why do you like these songs?"

"Well … they're unburdened by the constraints we have today. So much energy, emotion focused on feelings and relationships. Back then, before things fell apart, life was so …"

"Romantic?"

"Um … yes." She turned her attention to the device she was working on at the narrow desk beside her bed. I drifted into sleep.

• • •

The next week, I began to work as a physical therapist in Hanna's hospital. I had to remember not to encourage patients to exercise more, but instead to focus on stretches so they would retain mobility, if not strength. I was constantly hungry. But I wanted to keep fit, so I exercised. But during down times, I meditated and used biofeedback to lower my metabolism and conserve energy – and I slept a lot. Hanna nodded approvingly when I explained this. "I wish my husband could have done the same," she said. "Like all of us, he was constantly hungry. But somehow, he could never get used to it. 'My metabolism is too high,' he said. Then his immune system broke down and he got one illness after another. I begged, connived, pulled every string I could, to get him extra rations. But when some came, they didn't help. Those diseases had taken too much of a toll. He passed away less than two years ago."

For over a minute neither of us said anything. Then I asked if we could walk outside in the narrow courtyards between buildings and to some overlooks above the sea. Hanna agreed, but insisted we wear oxygen backpacks with snuggly fitting masks.

The second week, I had a day off. I took an oxygen backpack and began to explore south towards the station on the Long Island Expressway. After scrambling down a slope, pushing aside bushes and branches of stunted trees, and stumbling over the foundations of a once stately hillside home, I found what I was searching for — the foundations of my parents' house, my boyhood home.

Only one concrete corner was above water. Above that was the entrance to a storage shed, a cave, cut into the side of the hill and covered by a flat clearing that used to be our tennis court. A screen of leaves and creepers hid a recessed sliding steel door. I pulled away the vegetation. I remembered I could usually get the lock to open if I struck I laterally with a large flat stone. And it did this time, too – after over 222 years.

All the food on the shelves and in the freezer and refrigerator had decayed. But about ten bottles of wine looked possibly drinkable. And there was the aluminum dinghy with its outboard motor and a couple of oxygen tanks containing pure oxygen. My parents had been expert scuba divers and occasionally used pure oxygen during their dives. However, as I grew older and we used the dinghy less, my parents would drain all the gasoline from the motor after each use. They also bought a high tech 25-gallon airtight gasoline container that they flushed with helium each time they closed it so the gasoline would not deteriorate. I shook the tank. It was nearly full. The valves on the oxygen tanks looked intact.

As I left the shed, I noticed a groundhog emerging from a burrow above the corner foundation. It looked around, then another groundhog emerged. The first one advanced cautiously. The second one followed. Soon, they were playing and chasing each other all around.

I carried back one of the oxygen tanks, and when Hanna returned that evening, told her about the cave. The first thing she did was to check the oxygen level in my backpack.

"Oh no, it's so low!" she cried. "We only get these once every three months! They come from the mainland, and there're not enough there, either. They are so precious."

I brought out the oxygen tank and we examined its valves. Her face brightened. "This might work," she said. The next day she brought a connector from the hospital, and we refilled the tank I had drained.

"Let's top yours up," I said.

"Why?"

"So we can do something together, something fun."

"Like what?"

"Take the boat out."

"Eh?"

"I'm serious. For just a few hours, let's experience life a bit like what it used to be."

"What's the point of one senseless fling?"

"It's life as it was meant to be, not just for humans, but for all creatures. Life on earth flourished and advanced not because it adapted to constraints, but because it was able to use abundantly the resources this planet offered. Let's experience life as it should be. ... or are you afraid we'll be locked up if someone sees us out in the boat?"

"It used to be like that, during the first decades of the catastrophe. But everything's automated now. We know what almost every person on the planet is consuming. It's hard to cheat or hoard. Some elderly people walk around the apartments at odd hours just to make sure things are OK. That's all."

"It's June so the sun's rising early. It will be easy to launch the boat by my old house before dawn. We'll probably be back before anyone can notice."

•   •   •

The next Sunday just before 5 am, we crept down to the storage shed. I broke the seal on the large gasoline container and examined a cup of its contents. The gasoline looked and smelled fine, and I filled two portable cans.

Down to the water's edge we carried the dinghy, the outboard motor, the portable gasoline cans, the remaining oxygen tank in case we needed to replenish our backpacks, some buckwheat balls with insect paste inside, and a bottle of wine. With the two dinghy paddles we pushed off from shore a couple meters. I poured gasoline into the engine. I gave the pull cord a sharp tug. The engine coughed twice then purred to life, with only a few seconds of blue smoke as it cleared centuries old residue from its fuel lines and combustion chambers. Then it propelled us smoothly forward on the gasoline my parents had preserved so well.

"We'll stay close to shore," I reassured Hanna. "We're bringing enough gas to last five hours, and we're planning to be out for less than two."

We headed south past the train station and its tunnel emerging from the water, then rounded a point of land which used to be a hill overlooking Old Bethpage. It was just before sunrise.

We opened the bottle of wine to welcome the dawn. We took our first sips looking east anticipating the rising sun. But when we looked west, we saw thin vertical shards of orange-purple light suspended above the water. As we watched, these spikes of light extended downwards towards the ocean, and just as they touched the sea, the first sliver of the sun's globe appeared in the east. For a minute, we stared in awe at the towers of Manhattan rising out of the sea as they reflected the sun's first rays.

"Have you seen them up close?" I asked.

"Just once on a high school trip. There's an observation platform above the Brooklyn Bridge. When you look down, you see the submerged bridge towers. When you look across what used to be the East River, you see the massive towers rising from the ocean ... it's the most common destination for school field trips from all along the East Coast."

As we sipped more wine, the spires changed from red to orange to bright yellow before the reflected sunlight vanished.

"Where should we go next?"

"I'd like to see my apartment. But it's so far away, and we shouldn't be out long after sunrise."

"Let's see what our little boat can do," I said starting the engine and turning up the throttle. The boat responded well. The sea was calm, and we could go at a good clip without jarring bounces over waves.

"Isn't it fun to be out here like this? Here, give it a try," I said, motioning to Hanna to switch seats and take control of the motor.

She managed the throttle well, and we proceeded north along a channel between West Hills and Dix Hills to the east. Both islands were covered by similar tall, drab buildings built after the seas rose.

"These were all built pretty quickly?"

"Yes, over just a few decades about 70 years ago. Most people who used to live in Queens and Brooklyn fled to the mainland. But most other Long Island residents ended up on these two islands or on smaller islands just to the north — or on boats moored around them. Life was dreadful for the survivors. It was said that the dead were the lucky ones. But once the sea stopped rising, long term housing and workspaces had to be built. We couldn't pay much attention to aesthetics."

After about 45 minutes we turned east.

"Is that your apartment?"

"Oh, yeah. ... just another hermetically sealed tower covered with solar panels and square windows. Hey, what's that to the east? It looks like a French chateau surrounded by tall towers like mine."

It was the Oheka Castle, built during the First World War, one of the largest, most elegant private homes in

America. Part of the roof had fallen in, exposing bare timbers. Some of the windows were boarded up. Others were open holes in the walls. The stone balustrade at the edge of the eastern courtyard was crumbling.

"Seventy years ago, there was a big debate whether to tear it down and use the land for apartments, or to preserve it to let people know what luxury life was like," Hanna said. "The preservationists kept delaying destruction. Now that most people have a place to live, it probably will be saved, but there are no funds for restoration."

I tried to describe how it epitomized American luxury and status. But the only thing Hanna could relate it to were photos of European palaces like Versailles.

Gazing at the castle, we finished the bottle of wine. Then Hanna exclaimed, "It's past 6:30! We need to head back. People are getting up and looking out their windows."

"But you said it was OK."

"For the past 100 years, you've needed a permit to run any sort of gasoline motor. But those motors are so rare, no one issues permits any more. It's something we've forgotten about … but we can't attract attention."

She began to increase speed. I was seated in the front, looking forward. I slipped off my oxygen mask.

"What the hell are you doing!?" Hanna yelled, cutting the engine.

"I want to breathe naturally and feel the wind in my face. It won't kill me. I can manage some headache and nausea."

"Forget about headache and nausea. In seconds, you'll start feeling confused. Then you'll pass out. Then you'll die."

"People climb Everest without oxygen." But suddenly the horizon began undulating. I felt I was swaying more than the boat, and I couldn't remember what I wanted to say next. I slipped my mask back on. My mind cleared and I pretended I had not felt any symptoms. "People lived at 20,000 feet (6000 meters), two-thirds the height of Everest. We can adjust to low oxygen."

"Those people have genes that allow them to handle low oxygen. And no human was ever able to live for more than one or two years at 6000 meters. Climbers who scaled Everest without oxygen spent a long time adjusting to high altitudes, and they got back to low altitudes quickly."

"I saw a couple of ground hogs running around just above my old house. They were playing, having fun, not gasping for air. Life can adjust. We just have to try."

"Rodents are different from humans. I see rats around here. I guess after many deaths and many generations, they evolved, and the survivors are adapted to low oxygen. But I haven't seen any other animals out in the open."

Just then, a flock of waterfowl flew overhead, circled, and landed in the water about 50 meters away.

"I can't believe this," she said softly. "I've never seen birds before. ... Maybe life can adapt."

But having spent hours watching birds, I knew better. "They are Andean geese — adapted to live at high altitudes, like 3000 maybe even 6000 meters. Among all birds, it's easiest for them to adapt to the low oxygen around us."

"So we may see more of these, but not likely others?"

I nodded in response.

"Oh my God! It's going to be seven soon. We've got to get back, or we'll be spotted and questioned for sure."

She opened the throttle wide. I was now seated facing her, and the dinghy was going at maximum speed.

Maybe she was distracted thinking about the birds, maybe she was a bit tipsy from the wine. I definitely was not paying attention to what was in front. Suddenly, she cried, "JOHN, LOOK OUT LEFT!!" and swung the boat hard right. I glimpsed a jagged metal frame just left of our prow, no more than a meter above the water but with rusted arms extending over the water.

"GET DOWN!" I yelled, diving towards the bottom of the dinghy and managing to grab her arm and start pulling her down, when, with a loud bang and screech of metal against metal, the boat crashed into something underwater. My back was propelled against the seat and Hanna thrown against me. I felt a blow to my left side as the air was knocked out of my lungs. My life vest was torn open from back to front across my lower chest. I was bleeding.

Water was pouring into the dinghy through a gash in the bottom from front to back. Fortunately, whatever submerged metal that tore through had missed Hanna. The aluminum pontoon that formed the dinghy's left side was bashed in and open to water. Off our stern, the metal frame we had glimpsed had crumpled into the water, but I recognized it as a rusting cell phone tower.

Hanna and I were now clinging to the intact pontoon that formed the right side of the dinghy, the rest of which was submerged. She looked down and saw my torn life jacket and shirt and blood oozing into the water. I peered down and saw the roof of a large building. "We're at Saks Fifth Avenue," I gasped.

"John, you're losing it! Fifth Avenue is far away." Her hand was feeling my wound and then pressing tightly on it. She thought the lining around my lungs had been torn and was trying to prevent water from entering my chest. Tears were running down her face along with sea water.

"You're badly injured! Oh, I'm so sorry. I wasn't paying attention. Don't lose consciousness! Don't leave me now!"

I caught my breath and managed to speak calmly. "Just below us is the Walt Whitman shopping mall. We ran into an old cell phone tower atop the roof of a store called Saks Fifth Avenue. ... I think, I'm OK ... except it hurts down here when I breathe," I said, touching her hand pressed tightly over the wound.

The engine was pulling the stern of the boat underwater. I moved around Hanna to get close to it and began groping with my left hand to release the clamp. Hanna thought I was releasing my grip on the boat. "John, stay with me!" she yelled. She was pulling up on my life jacket, trying to hoist me on top of the pontoon.

"I don't feel short of breath. I can breathe OK. But the motor is pulling us down." And with that, I managed to loosen the clamps, using my foot to ease it over the stern and let it sink.

Hanna scrutinized my movements, finally concluding I probably didn't have a punctured chest. "Let's change life jackets," she insisted. "Yours is too badly torn right where you need projection. Now cinch it tightly down so there's pressure right over the wound."

We were about half a mile from shore. With each of us holding one side of the right pontoon, we kicked towards shore, still wearing our oxygen back packs and masks. But it took too much effort to push the stricken dinghy. Hanna was tiring and the pain over my ribs grew more intense. We let the dinghy go.

Then, having covered barely a third of the distance to shore, yellow lights on our masks flashed warning we were low on oxygen. We were breathing so hard that we had nearly depleted our supply. Our backup, the large cylinder, had sunk. We tried to kick less and glide more, but without kicking the current was pulling us farther from shore. Then with a third of the way still to go, a red light on my mask flashed indicating I had only five minutes of oxygen remaining, then the same light flashed on Hanna's mask. We decided to swim as fast as we could.

It happened that the closest shoreline was right below Hanna's apartment. But to reach the entrance, we had to climb a steep slope.

As I neared shore, everything became blurry. I was breathing fast. I sensed Hanna pulling me then dragging me out of the water. I must have come to seconds later. Hanna was sharing her oxygen mask with me.

"There's still a bit left in mine," she said. "I think I see a path. Follow me."

She led the way, I followed closely so we could share the remaining oxygen. Then she began to stumble and veer back towards the ocean. I had to grab her to prevent her from running into a tree. "I can't go on," she murmured. I hoisted her on my back, holding her high enough so I could bend her head over my shoulder and keep sharing whatever oxygen remained and pressed up the hill.

I remember little of that last climb. Branches struck my face and arms as I tried to shield Hanna's head. I felt separated from my body, floating above it, but it consisted only of legs trudging uphill. The last thing I remember was a flat clearing with green grass, falling, then darkness. Hanna related what happened next:

"I was walking in an open field with a bright blue sky above. I saw my husband clothed in white, and we walked together. There was no need for masks. We could breathe the air. Suddenly the earth shook and my husband began to fade.

'You need to take care of John,' he said. I opened my eyes. We were face down on the grass next to each other. Twenty meters away was a door to my apartment complex. I had to summon all my concentration and strength to drag myself to the door, lift myself to the iris scanner, and pull the door open a few centimeters. I stuck a hand through the opening and began to breathe the oxygen rich air. This gave me enough strength to pull the rest of my body through. I wanted to go back and pull you in, but I couldn't even crawl.

How long before I regain enough strength to pull you? I asked myself. Instead, I dragged myself to the elevator and managed to get an express ride to my floor. I crawled to my apartment, managed to open it, grabbed the other oxygen cylinder with the connector device and crawled back to the elevator. By the time I reached the ground floor, I could stand. I dragged the oxygen cylinder along the corridor and out the door to where you were lying."

When I came to, Hanna was lying on the grass, her face close to mine with the tube between our noses. The cylinder valve was fully open, and oxygen was rushing into our lungs. "Let's get inside," she said. We crawled together towards the door, dragging the tank between us.

After we entered, we sprawled on the floor by the doorway. A middle-aged couple on their way to the eatery serving its Sunday morning special of pancakes with sweetened algae jelly walked by. "Hey, are you two all right?"

"We're OK," I heard myself saying, wondering if it were true.

"Just coming off a hard Saturday night, right? Nice to know people can still have fun together."

"Say, aren't you Dr. Kovacs?" the man asked.

"Uh, yes,"

"Looks like you and your friend had a real night on the town, a big adventure."

"Kinda of ... Unexpected."

"Let's get out of here," we said to each other as they walked away.

Hanna opened the door of her apartment and we both sank to the floor. But she rose, listened to our lungs, measured our blood pressures and oxygen levels, and had us take dexamethasone pills. We dragged pillows and blankets onto the floor and slept. But within an hour, Hanna awoke to clean the wound over my ribs, anesthetize the skin and carefully sew the wound shut. Then we slept again.

A week later, I crept over to my parents' storeroom and safely disposed of the remaining gasoline. Then I took the empty oxygen cylinder from Hanna's apartment to a recycling area (we had used the remaining oxygen in it to replenish our oxygen backpacks) and dropped it into a bin for large metal objects. Later that day, Hanna helped me make a copy of the photo of Lydia, Jeremy, Heather, and Yvonne, all gathered around my Wilton kitchen table. We displayed it on the wall of our apartment, alongside a photo of her deceased husband, Sebastian.

ABOUT THE AUTHOR

Kellyn Solvera worked in China, Japan, and near Washington DC. Kellyn now writes and practices primary care medicine in the Pacific Northwest.

YOU MIGHT ALSO ENJOY

CHOOSE YOUR TRUTH
by Jo Miles

Truth is obsolete. May the best lies win.

DENISOVAN HARMONY
by DJ Cockburn

You're watching the first Homo denisova to walk the earth in a hundred and fifty centuries grope their way into adolescence.

SAYING GOODBYE
by J Dark

A young girl, searching for the parents who abandoned her, discovers that some answers only lead to more questions.

Available in digital and trade paperback editions from
Water Dragon Publishing
waterdragonpublishing.com

www.ingramcontent.com/pod-product-compliance
Lightning Source LLC
Chambersburg PA
CBHW021602310726
48972CB00003B/905